There is no one method or technique that is the ONLY way to learn to read. Children learn in a variety of ways. **Read with me** is an enjoyable and uncomplicated scheme that will give your child reading confidence. Through exciting stories about Kate, Tom and Sam the dog, **Read with me**:

- *teaches the first 300 key words (75% of our everyday language) plus 500 additional words*

- *stimulates a child's language and imagination through humorous, full colour illustration*

- *introduces situations and events children can relate to*

- *encourages and develops conversation and observational skills*

- *support material includes Practice and Play Books, Flash Cards, Book and Cassette Packs*

Always praise and encourage as you go along. Keep your reading sessions short and stop immediately if your child loses interest.

Published by Ladybird Books Ltd
80 Strand London WC2R 0RL
A Penguin Company
7 9 10 8 6

Printed in Italy

Read with me
Lost in
Piper's park

by WILLIAM MURRAY
stories by JILL CORBY
illustrated by JON DAVIS

Tom is looking at his mother cleaning the room. First she makes the beds with clean things. Then she cleans everything in the room. She is doing a lot of work.

"Why are you doing so much cleaning today, Mum ?" Tom asks her.

"Granny and Grandpa are coming to stay," she tells him, "and I must get everything ready."

Tom looks at her getting everything clean. He thinks for a little time and then he says, "May I get some flowers from the garden and put them in a clean vase for Granny and Grandpa?"

"Yes," says his mum. "They will like that very much."

So Tom goes out into the garden to get some flowers.

"What are you doing?" Kate asks him. He tells her that Granny and Grandpa are coming to stay and that Mum said that he could get some flowers to put in their room.

"I like Granny and Grandpa," Kate says. "I will help Mum with the cleaning."

Kate tells Tom that they could put the flowers in the blue vase that was Mum's birthday present. When they have put the flowers in the vase, Tom says he will take them up to Granny and Grandpa's room.

"Their train will be in soon," Dad tells them, "and we must go and meet them."

Tom and Kate get into the car, but their mother stays at home. She wants the dinner to be ready when they get back.

So Tom and Kate go off in the car with their father to meet the train. As soon as they get there, they see the train coming.

"Keep back please, Tom," Dad says. "Here comes the train now."

They all stay well back as the train comes to a stop.

"I can see them," shouts Tom. "They are down there."

So they all go over to meet Granny and Grandpa.

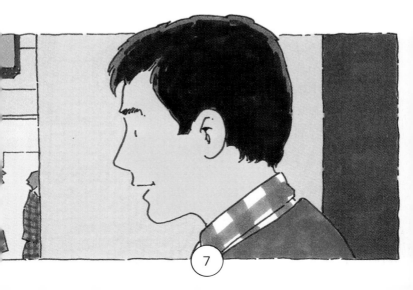

Grandpa and Granny are very pleased to see them.

"Thank you for coming to meet us," Grandpa says.

"How are you all?" Granny asks.

"We are all very well, thank you," Dad tells her.

Then Dad says that it is lovely to see them again and he looks at all their bags. Tom takes a bag and Kate takes one.

"I'll take these big bags for you," says Dad.

"Look at Sam," Kate says. "He wants to help as well."

They take all the bags out to the car.
Dad puts them all in the back. Then
they all get in and away they go.

"We will just be back in time for
dinner," Dad tells them.

When they get home, they see Mum
outside.

"Out we all get," says Dad. "And I
will take the bags out of the back of
the car."

"It's lovely to see you again," Mum tells Grandpa and Granny. "Come on inside."

They all go in and Mum asks Tom and Kate if they had to wait a long time for the train. Kate tells her that the train came in just as they got there.

"We came in right on time, too," Grandpa says.

"It didn't take very long at all," Granny tells them. "And it's lovely to be here again."

Mum takes them up to their room and tells them that dinner will be ready soon. She puts everything on the table and tells everyone to come and sit down.

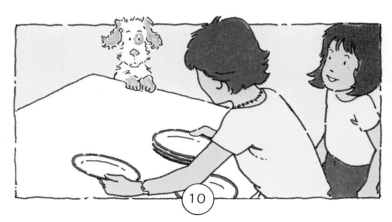

They all sit round the table to eat their dinner. They talk about all the things that they have been doing. Dad asks Granny and Grandpa what they would like to do in the next day or two.

"Could we go to Piper's park, do you think?" Granny asks.

"Yes, Piper's park! That would be fantastic," say Tom and Kate.

They have to go to Piper's park by train, as there is not room in the car for all of them and Sam. Dad tells them that it won't take very long to get to Piper's park, as the train goes faster than the car.

"And we won't have to park the car," he says. "When we get off at the station, we are right by the entrance to Piper's park."

They walk from the station to the entrance, but there are so many boys and girls with their mothers and fathers, that everyone has to wait for tickets to get in. They don't have to wait for very long before they are at the entrance and can buy their tickets.

Dad tells them that the tickets give them rides on everything in Piper's park.

"As many rides as we like?" Tom asks.

"Yes," says Mum. "As many rides as you want."

"Where shall we start?" Kate and Tom look round at all the things.

"Let's have a go on that big wheel first," says Kate.

"Yes," Tom tells them. "It's over there."

They all go over to the big wheel.

"We will sit on this seat," Kate tells Grandpa. "And Tom can sit with Granny on that seat."

Mum and Dad don't go on the big wheel as they have to look after Sam.

14

Then the big wheel starts off and they go high up, as high as the trees.

"Now we can see over the top of the trees," Tom tells Granny.

"I can see right over the top of the trees to the water over there," Kate says. "It's windy up here, very windy."

"Look," says Tom. "There are some boats on the water."

They look down at all the things that they will be doing soon.

Then they start to go down again.

"I like going round on this big wheel," Kate tells them.

When the big wheel stops, Kate gets out of her seat. She goes over to her mum and tells her how windy it was at the top of the big wheel.

"Just look at me. I didn't know it was so windy up there," she says, and they all laugh.

"May we have another go?" she asks.

"Not just now," says Mum.

"Would you like a cup of tea, now?" Mum asks Granny and Grandpa. "We can sit at that table and have a cup of tea."

Tom and Kate don't want a cup of tea, so they go to climb up the big hill to the top of the slide.

"We can see you from here," Dad tells them.

"Yes," says Mum. "Climb where we can see you, please."

So Tom and Kate start to climb the hill. When they get to the top of the slide, they can see the others with another cup of tea. They talk and laugh as they let go and slide down. They climb up and slide down again and again.

Tom and Kate run over to the others.

"When I was at the top of the hill," Tom tells them, "I could see right over to a little train. Please can we have a go on it?"

"Right," says Dad. "We'll go and find the train."

"The station was over that way," Tom tells them.

They find the station and get on the train. There are lots of seats.

Sam can have a ride as well. He sits on a seat just like the others, and the train starts off.

First, they go into the gardens.

Granny says, ''I don't think that these flowers are as lovely as the ones that you two put in my room at home.''

Kate looks at all the flowers. She can see that there are many more flowers in this garden. These flowers are best, she thinks.

The little train goes round by the water. They look at all the boats on the water. It's a bit windy.

"Look," Kate tells them. "All the boats are made to look like birds. Please may we have a go on a bird boat?" she asks. "They look lovely on the water."

Dad tells them that they can get off at the station soon. Then they can walk back to the boats and have a ride.

"Will there be room for all of us in one boat?" asks Tom.

Dad tells him that he thinks there will be, but that he doesn't know if Sam can ride in any of the boats.

"I am going to ask that man over there," he says.

So they all walk over to the man who looks after the boats. He tells them that Sam can go in a boat if he is good.

"He is always good," Tom tells the man.

"Always?" asks the man, with a laugh.

"Yes, always," says Tom.

The man says that they may ride in any of the boats. They look at all the boats on the water. Which one is the best?

"I like this red, brown and blue one best," says Kate. "May we all ride in this bird, please?" she asks.

They all start to get in.

"Sit on any seat you like," the man tells them.

"I am going to sit here, on this white seat, with Granny," Kate says. "And Tom, you can sit on that brown seat there, with Grandpa."

They laugh at Kate as she tells everyone where to sit.

"How does our bird know where to go?" Tom asks. "We are not making it go are we?"

"That man over there is making it go. He looks after all the boats. He sees that they don't bump into one another," Mum tells him.

"It wouldn't be good at all for them to go round and bump," Tom says. "The birds do not like any bumps."

After they have been for the ride in the bird boat, they all want to sit on a seat under the tree.

Granny says that it is not so hot under the tree. But Tom and Kate don't want to sit down. They always want to go and play.

"Only children can go up that net over there," Tom tells his mum. "Only we can climb it. Please can we go up the net with all those children?"

Tom starts to climb up the net with the other children. Kate is not happy about going up the net.

"I am up here," Tom shouts to Kate. "Climb up here. You can't fall down. There's a safety net."

Kate looks at the big net. Then she sees the safety net.

"I can't fall down with that safety net there, so here I come Tom."

Kate climbs up to the top with Tom and they laugh.

"There, we didn't fall down, did we?" says Kate.

Tom says, "If we did we would only fall into the safety net."

At the top, they find a long slide to take them down. As soon as they get off the slide they go back for another turn. Every time they slide down, they always go faster and faster.

They hear Dad tell them to come back now, as they want to walk over to the gardens. At the same time, they hear some music.

"Can you hear the music, Granny?" Kate asks. "I think it's coming from over there."

They look over to where the music is coming from and they see lots of clowns walking and jumping along. Some of the clowns are making music. They stop to look at them.

"Just look at that clown with a white face and a brown hat, going along on only one wheel," says Kate.

"How can he ride with only one wheel?" she asks. "Why doesn't he fall off, Mum?"

Mum tells her that the clown
did fall off at first.
He had to ride for
a long time to be
so good at it.

Tom likes the very tall clown in red and white. He starts to walk along just like the tall clown.

Then all the children look at the clowns making music.

"That green clown is playing a trumpet just like mine," Tom tells Kate.

"And the orange clown has some cymbals like yours," says Kate, "but yours are not as big as his."

"I like the red and yellow clown playing the big drum," Tom says. "I am playing a drum as well."

And he laughs as he walks along by the clown playing the drum.

They look at the clown playing with the balls. Round and round they go.

"How does he keep them all going round?" Kate asks her dad.

Just then Granny walks on a stone and she falls over. Mum and Dad help her up and take her to a seat.

"Oh dear! Oh dear, it's my foot," she tells them. "It must have been that stone over there."

Granny sits down on the seat.

"Oh dear, my foot does hurt," she tells them.

"Just stay on this seat and I will go and get some help," Dad says, and off he goes.

"I will see if I can walk now," Granny says.

She gets up to walk.

"Oh dear, no," she tells them. "It hurts too much. But it doesn't hurt when I am sitting down." So she sits down and waits.

Soon Dad comes back with the First Aid man. He looks at Granny's foot and asks her where it hurts. Then the First Aid man opens his bag and takes out a bandage. They all look at the First Aid man as he puts the bandage round and round Granny's foot.

"I did it on a little stone," she tells him.

"There you are," the First Aid man says. "Walk on your foot now, and see how it is."

Granny gets up and walks about.

"This bandage is lovely," she tells him.
"My foot doesn't hurt any more. I
won't walk on any more stones."

The First Aid man goes away to put
another bandage on a boy who has
had a bump.

Granny stays sitting for a bit and then
she gets up to walk again.

"It doesn't hurt at all now," she tells
them. "So where shall we go next?"

Then Kate says, "Where is Tom? I can't see him anywhere."

"Oh dear," Grandpa says. "Where can he have gone?"

"Tom was looking at the clowns with us," says Mum.

"We shall have to look everywhere for him," Dad tells them.

So they start to look everywhere that they have been.

BUT YOU KNOW WHERE TOM IS, DON'T YOU? YOU CAN SEE HIM GOING OFF.

They look for Tom by the hill and by the net. They go to the little train and they look at the table where they had tea. But Tom is not anywhere.

Granny asks Mum, "Where can Tom be? Oh dear, what can he be doing?"

So what did Tom get up to?

You saw him walking along by the clown playing the big drum. Tom was playing his drum, just like the clown. And then he went to play his trumpet by the clown with the big trumpet. Then he went to play the cymbals just like the clown with the big cymbals.

When he had done all that, he saw
the very tall clown, so he made
himself tall. He made himself as tall
as he could and went walking along
with him. But Tom could not keep up
with the tall clown.

So then Tom went to the clown who could ride on only one wheel. This clown was so good at riding it that he did not fall off at all. Tom was very happy with all the clowns.

Then the music was over and all the other children went back to their mothers and fathers.

Tom could not see his mum or his dad. Then he was not so happy. He was not happy at all.

"What am I going to do now?" he said to himself. "Where can they be?"

Just then the clown with the white face and brown hat jumped down from his bike and came over to Tom.

"Don't you know where your mum and dad are?" he asked.

"No," said Tom. "They were over there but now I can't see them anywhere."

"Right," said the clown. "How about riding with me and we will go and find them. They will be looking round for you, too."

So Tom and the clown with the white face went off to find the others.

They came to the hill and looked but they were not there. They came to the net and looked but they were not there. They were not on the seat and they were not where they had had a cup of tea. Now Tom didn't know where to look next and he started to get a bit sad. Where could he look now?

Where are the others looking?

They walk to a high hill where they can see over the top of everyone. They all look one way and Sam looks the other way. Sam can see Tom coming. He barks at him and Tom hears him bark. Then the others hear Tom shout. They are very pleased and surprised to see him with the clown.

Sam barks and barks.

"Sam saw Tom first," Kate says.

"Where have you been, Tom?" asks Dad.

Tom tells them where he has been. "I saw the music clowns, so I went down there with them. But I won't do it again."

Tom tells them all about it. Kate asks the clown if she may have a ride. So the clown helps her up. Kate laughs as they go round and round.

Mum and Dad say thank you very much to the clown, and Kate says thank you for the ride. Then it's time to go home.

They walk back by the gardens. They see the little train that they went on and the bird boat.

Dad tells them that they must walk faster if they are going to get to the station in time.

When they get to the station entrance, the train is just coming in and Dad runs to get the tickets.

Look at the picture and talk about the answers.

What is each clown playing?

What is the other clown doing?

What was the clown with the white face and brown hat riding?

LADYBIRD READING SCHEMES

Ladybird reading schemes are suitable for use with any other method of learning to read.

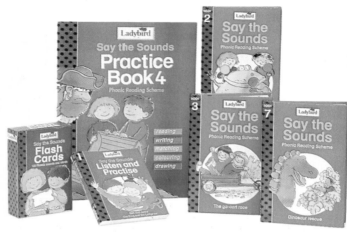

Say the Sounds

Ladybird's **Say the Sounds** graded reading scheme is a *phonics* scheme. It teaches children the sounds of individual letters and letter combinations, enabling them to tackle new words by building them up as a blend of smaller units.

There are 8 titles in this scheme:

1 **Rocket to the jungle**
2 **Frog and the lollipops**
3 **The go-cart race**
4 **Pirate's treasure**
5 **Humpty Dumpty and the robots**
6 **Flying saucer**
7 **Dinosaur rescue**
8 **The accident**

Support material available: Practice Books, Double Cassette Pack, Flash Cards